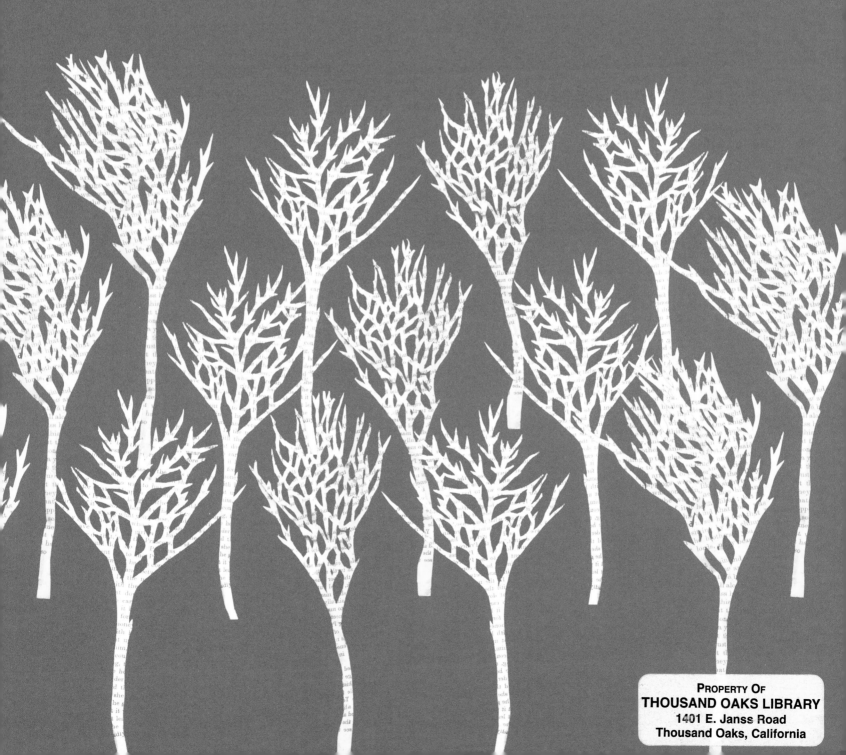

The Fairy-Tale Princess

The Fairy-Tale Princess

Seven Classic Stories
from the Enchanted Forest

SU BLACKWELL

Retellings by Wendy Jones

Thames & Hudson

Contents

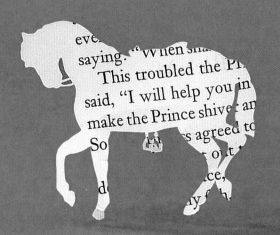

Cinderella

ONCE UPON A TIME, there was a young girl whose mother fell sick. Before the mother died, she told her sweet-natured daughter, "Be good and you will always be protected."

Now the girl's father was rich and he soon married again. His second wife was a haughty woman with two vile daughters who were hard of heart. No sooner was the wedding over than the new wife showed her true colors. She gave all the hard work around the house to her new stepdaughter. Every day, the girl washed the pots, swept the floors and cleaned the hearth.

The poor girl never complained. When the housework was done, she tucked herself away in the fireplace to keep warm, among the cinders. That's why her stepsisters called her Cinderella. Yet, even in her dirty clothes, Cinderella was one hundred times kinder and more beautiful than her stepsisters.

It happened that the king was holding a ball and he invited all the girls in the kingdom. When the two stepsisters received their invitations, they were delighted. They spoke of nothing else and were always looking in the mirror. On the night of the ball, they shouted at Cinderella, "Comb our hair! Brush our shoes! Fasten our corsets!"

Cinderella was patient and did as she was told. But she begged her stepmother to be allowed to go to the ball, too.

"You are covered in dust and dirt, and you have no fine clothes," said her stepmother. "Everyone would laugh at you!"

The house was empty as Cinderella went about her chores, and she wept as she did so.

"What's the matter, child?" said a kindly voice. Cinderella's fairy godmother had appeared as if out of nowhere.

"I want…" Cinderella was crying too hard to speak.

"You want to go to the ball," said her godmother. "First, go to the garden and pick me a pumpkin."

Cinderella picked the plumpest pumpkin she could find. Her godmother struck the pumpkin with her wand and it changed into a golden coach.

"Fetch me mice from the mousetrap."

As the mice dashed out of the trap, the godmother tapped each one lightly with her wand and it turned into a white horse. Soon the golden coach had six fine white horses.

"Next, go and see if there are any rats in the rat-trap," said the godmother. "A rat would make a splendid coachman."

Cinderella found three fat rats in the rat-trap. One had particularly long whiskers. The godmother tapped this rat with her wand and it changed into a coachman with the most magnificent moustache you ever did see.

Finally, she tapped her wand on Cinderella's rags, which changed into a white dress that sparkled in the moonlight. Then she gave Cinderella the prettiest pair of glass slippers.

"Be home by midnight," warned her godmother. "If you stay one moment longer, your coach will turn into a pumpkin, your horses to mice, your coachman to a rat and your dress to rags."

"I promise," said Cinderella. And she left for the ball.

Yellow feet a-quiver,
went in two again, and they were in a worse plight than ever.

At the palace, the king's son was told that a mysterious princess had arrived, and he ran to meet her. The prince led Cinderella into the ballroom. When the guests saw her, silence descended. The dancing stopped. The fiddlers forgot to ply their bows. Everyone gazed in wonder at this unknown beauty. Cinderella's stepsisters did not even recognize the girl in the sparkling white dress. They thought that she must be a princess from far away in another kingdom.

The prince took Cinderella by the hand and danced only with her and no other all night. He never let go of her hand.

Suddenly Cinderella heard the chimes of the clock striking a quarter to twelve. "Oh!" she exclaimed. "It's late! I must go!" She made a deep curtsey to the prince. Then she ran as quickly as she could to her coach and horses to take her back home.

As Cinderella rushed down the palace staircase, one foot slipped out of its glass slipper. She hurried on, leaving it behind.

The next day the prince made an announcement.

"I shall marry the girl whose foot fits this glass slipper."

The prince traveled the kingdom trying the slipper on all the princesses, then all the duchesses, then all the ladies. But the slipper fit none of them. As the stepsisters waited their turn, they spoke of nothing else. Cinderella washed, swept and cleaned.

At last the prince brought the slipper for the sisters to try on. First, it was the elder sister's turn. She pushed and pushed but the slipper didn't fit.

"It fits perfectly," said her mother.

"It does not!" said the prince.

Then the younger sister tried. She pushed and pushed but the slipper didn't fit

"It fits perfectly," said her mother.

"It does not!" said the prince. "Have you no other daughter?"

"No," said the stepmother. "Only a servant who cleans the kitchen and sweeps the floor."

"I wish to see her," requested the prince.

"Oh, no," the stepmother replied. "She is much too dirty."

But the prince insisted. Cinderella washed the ashes from her face and curtseyed before the prince. She sat on a stool and slipped her foot into the glass slipper. It fit like a glove.

At that very moment, Cinderella's fairy godmother appeared as if out of nowhere. She tapped Cinderella's rags with her wand and at once they turned into a white dress that sparkled in the sunshine. When Cinderella rose up, the prince knew her immediately.

"You are my true bride," he cried.

Cinderella's stepmother and stepsisters were horrified and became pale with rage. But the prince had eyes only for Cinderella, whom he thought more beautiful than ever.

Cinderella and her prince went in a horse-drawn carriage to the palace, where they were married and lived happily ever after.

The Frog Prince

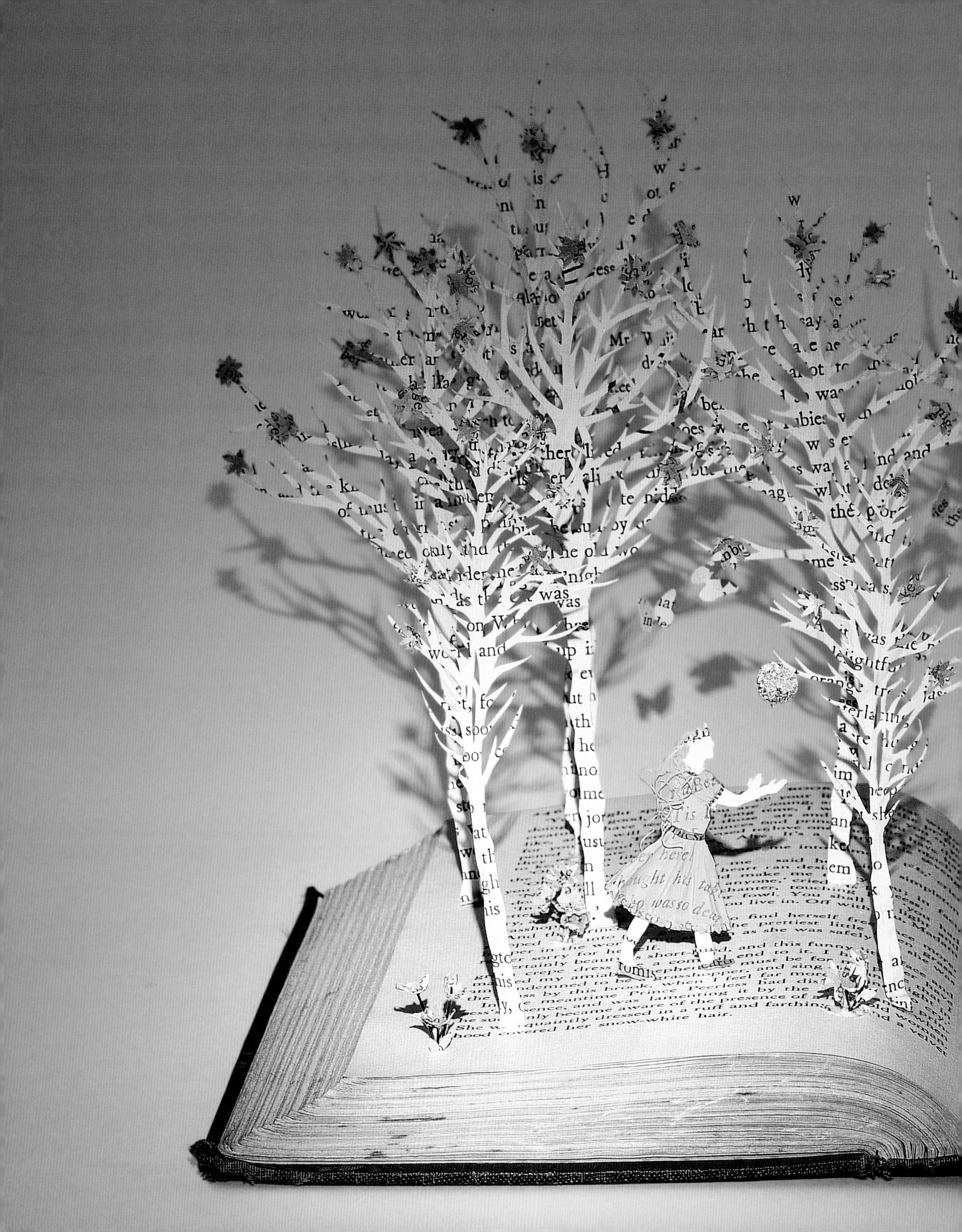

ONCE UPON A TIME, a princess was walking through a wood playing with a golden ball. She delighted in throwing the ball carelessly into the air and catching it, but then she threw the ball very high in the air. *Splash!* It fell into a deep, dark well.

As the princess sat weeping, a clammy fat frog appeared.

"Don't be sad, princess," croaked the frog.

"Go away, disgusting frog!" cried the princess.

"But I can help you," said the frog. "I will dive down for your ball if you promise to let me sit beside you at dinner, eat from your silver plate and sleep in your bed."

The princess so loved her golden ball that she agreed. The frog fetched the ball from the bottom of the well and the princess skipped home.

"Wait for me," cried the frog, but the princess didn't stop. She had already forgotten the frog.

The next day, there were three knocks on the palace door. The princess saw the frog and slammed the door shut.

"Who was that?" asked the king.

"Only a silly frog. I promised I would let him stay if he found my golden ball."

"My dear, we must all keep our promises," said the king. He opened the door for the frog, who hopped and plopped across the floor to the chair.

"Please lift me up," croaked the frog, but the princess didn't want to touch him.

"My dear, we must all keep our promises," said the king, so the princess reluctantly lifted the frog onto the table.

"Please push your silver plate closer," croaked the frog.

The princess was particularly fond of white meringues and didn't want to share hers with a frog.

"My dear, we must all keep our promises," said the king. And so the princess slowly pushed the silver plate closer to the frog.

"Please take me upstairs to bed," croaked the frog. At this, the princess burst into tears.

"The frog helped you when you were in need," said the king. "You must help him now. It is your duty."

So the princess picked up the frog with two fingers, carried him to her bedroom and dropped him onto her clean white pillow. Then she got into bed, balancing on the very edge so as not to touch the clammy frog.

In the morning, the frog was gone.

"Thank goodness for that!" she thought.

But that evening there were three knocks at the door. It was rice pudding for dinner, which the princess didn't much care for, so she pushed her silver plate towards the frog.

Then she carried the frog to bed, put him on her pillow and, in the morning, he was gone.

"Oh, where is he?" she said.

On the third evening, the frog fell into the soup and that made the princess laugh. She carried him to her bedroom, where she washed and dried him. Then she placed him carefully on her pillow, blew him a kiss and said, "Goodnight."

In the morning, the princess awoke hoping that the frog might still be there. And he was! As the first rays of sunshine came through the window, the frog gave a huge leap to the end of the bed and as he landed, he turned into a handsome prince.

"Oh!" exclaimed the princess.

"A wicked witch cast a spell on me," explained the prince. "She turned me into a frog. I couldn't escape from the deep dark well until someone became my friend. Your kindness has broken the spell."

It came to pass that the frog prince married the princess. Every day, they sat beside each other at dinner and ate from the same silver plate. They lived happily ever after.

The Twelve Dancing Princesses

ONCE THERE WAS a king who had twelve beautiful daughters, who all loved to dance. The twelve princesses slept in twelve beds in one bedroom. At night, the king bolted their door but every morning their shoes had been worn to shreds. The king couldn't understand why and his twelve mischievous daughters wouldn't tell him.

The king proclaimed, "Any man who tells me where my daughters dance at night may choose a princess for his wife and shall be king when I die. But any man who tries and fails after three nights will be banished from my kingdom."

A prince soon came to try his luck. That night he watched and waited outside the princesses' bedroom, but his eyes grew heavy and he fell asleep. When he woke in the morning, the princesses' shoes were in tatters. On the second night and third night, the prince slept too, so the king banished him.

Ten other princes tried and failed and all were banished.

Later, a soldier wounded from battle arrived in the kingdom. He was poor but kind and handsome. An old woman asked him where he was going.

"I don't know," he laughed, "but I should like to discover where the princesses dance so one day I can be king!"

The old woman was as wise as she was magical. She lowered her voice and said, "Then you must not drink the wine the princesses bring you, but pretend to be asleep." She gave him a cloak and said, "When you wear this, you will be invisible and can follow the princesses wherever they go."

The soldier thanked the old lady and rushed to the king.

That evening the soldier sat on a chair outside the princesses' bedroom. The eldest princess gave him a cup of wine, but the soldier had fastened a sponge under his chin and the wine ran down into the sponge so he didn't drink a drop. The soldier pretended to go to sleep.

The twelve princesses heard his snoring and laughed.

The eldest princess said, "He too will be banished." So skipping and twirling, the princesses prepared for a night of dancing.

"I don't know why," said the youngest princess, "but I feel as if misfortune will befall us tonight."

"You are young and foolish," said the eldest princess. "The soldier has drunk deeply of the sleeping potion. He won't stir."

Then the eldest sister knocked on her bed and it sank down into the earth. The twelve princesses skipped lightly hand in hand down a staircase into a secret tunnel, the eldest first in a gown of emerald green, the youngest last in a gown of lilac. The soldier threw on the cloak of invisibility and followed. But he accidentally trod on the gown of the youngest.

"I don't know why," she cried, "but I think that someone took hold of my gown!"

"Don't be foolish," said the eldest. "It's only a nail in the wall."

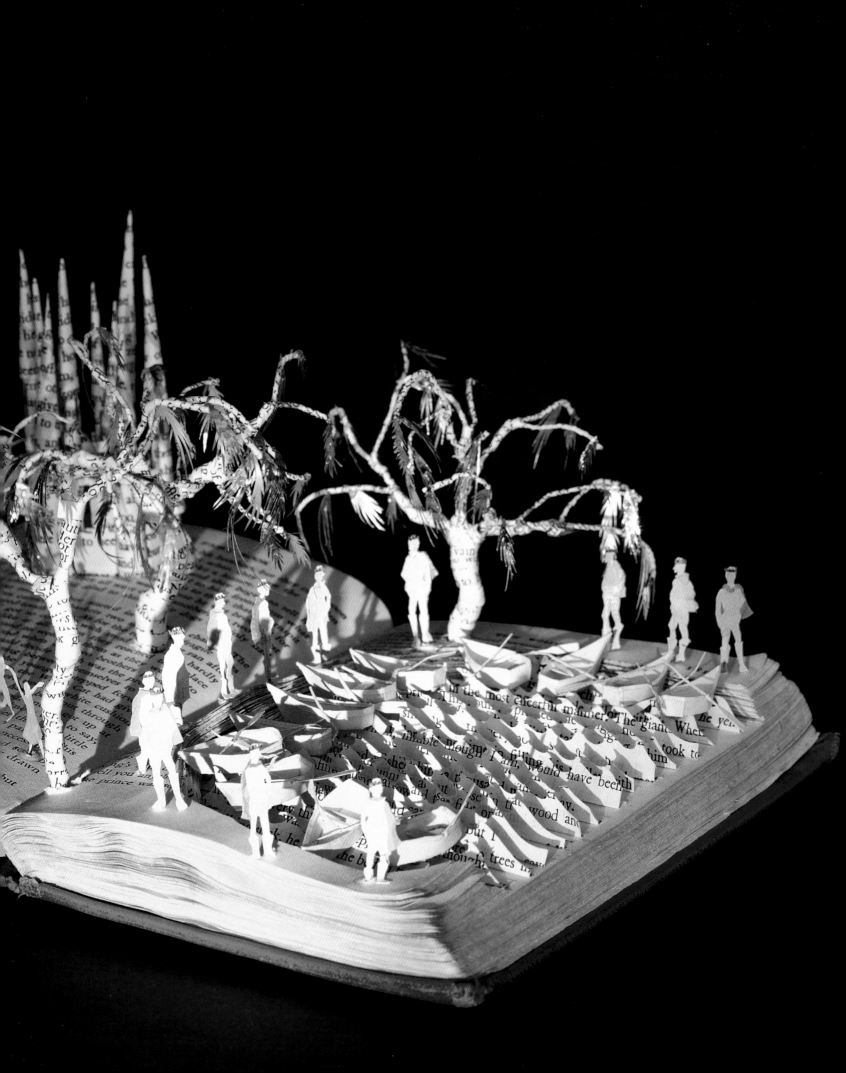

At the bottom of the stairs, there was a secret underground kingdom, with glistening trees and a shimmering lake.

The soldier thought, "I will take a token to show the king." So he broke off a twig from a silver tree.

Hearing the crack, the youngest princess started. "I don't know why, but I heard a strange noise," she cried.

The eldest princess said, "Don't be foolish. It is only a bird."

The princesses came to a golden tree and then a diamond one. The soldier broke off a twig from both and each time the youngest princess jumped in terror.

Then they came to the shore of a great lake where twelve princes waited by twelve rowing boats. On the other side of the lake, there was a splendid castle, from which came the sound of trumpets and drums.

Each prince rowed a princess across the lake. The soldier stepped into the same boat as the youngest princess.

"The boat feels much heavier tonight," remarked the prince.

"I wonder why?" replied the youngest princess.

Inside the castle, the twelve princesses waltzed with their princes. The soldier danced unseen. The princesses spun and twirled until their shoes were worn to shreds. At three o'clock in the morning, they returned home.

This time the soldier hid in the boat of the eldest princess and then ran on ahead until he reached the castle. He removed his cloak of invisibility, sat in his chair and pretended to snore.

When the sisters returned, the eldest said, "See, now all is safe." And the exhausted princesses fell fast asleep.

The soldier decided that he wanted to see more of the adventure. He went with the princesses on the second night and the third night. Everything happened just as before, and the princesses danced and danced until their shoes were worn to shreds. On the third night, the soldier took away a golden cup as a token of the underground castle.

After the third night, the king asked the solider, "Where do my daughters dance at night?"

"With twelve princes in a magical castle in an underground kingdom, Your Highness," the soldier answered. He showed the king the silver, gold and diamond twigs, and the golden cup.

The king asked his daughters, "Is this how you wear your dancing shoes to shreds?'

The twelve princesses knew that they had been discovered. The youngest princess wept. Ten of her sisters looked upset, but the eldest sister appeared thoughtful.

"Which of my daughters will you choose for your wife?" the king asked the soldier.

"The eldest," he replied, "because she is clever and beautiful." They were married that very day. And when the old king died, the soldier and his dancing princess became king and queen.

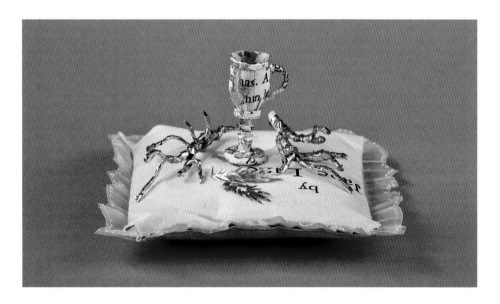

The Princess
and the Pea

ONCE LONG, LONG AGO, there was a wonderful and particularly handsome prince who wanted to marry a princess. But – and this was very important – she had to be a real princess. Not a silly princess, not a haughty one and not a mean one, either. A true princess. So he set out on a quest to find one.

He traveled all over the world, across many great lands, and he climbed mighty mountains – for he was fearless at climbing. He searched everywhere. He looked in castles and fine palaces, by rivers and streams, in gardens and in forests. He even looked under weeping willows and on desert islands.

The prince found plenty of princesses, lots of them, all over the place, but he could never be sure if they were real princesses or not. There was always something not as it should be. Some were silly, some were haughty and some were mean. So at last his quest came to an end and he wearily wended his way home. He was most downhearted, almost brokenhearted, because he did so want to find a real princess.

One evening, as the prince was sitting in the palace with his parents, there was a terrible storm. The thunder clapped. The lightning flashed. And it rained and it rained and it rained. Suddenly, in the moment between a mighty crack of lightning and a deafening clap of thunder, there was a knock – just a simple tap, tap, tap – on the palace gates.

"Who could that be?" asked the old king, and he went to find out.

Standing there in the pouring rain in the middle of the raging storm was a princess. But goodness, what a sight she was! The rain poured down from her head to her toes. It ran in rivulets from her hair, trickled down into her dress and dripped into her shoes like a waterfall. Still, she declared she was a real princess.

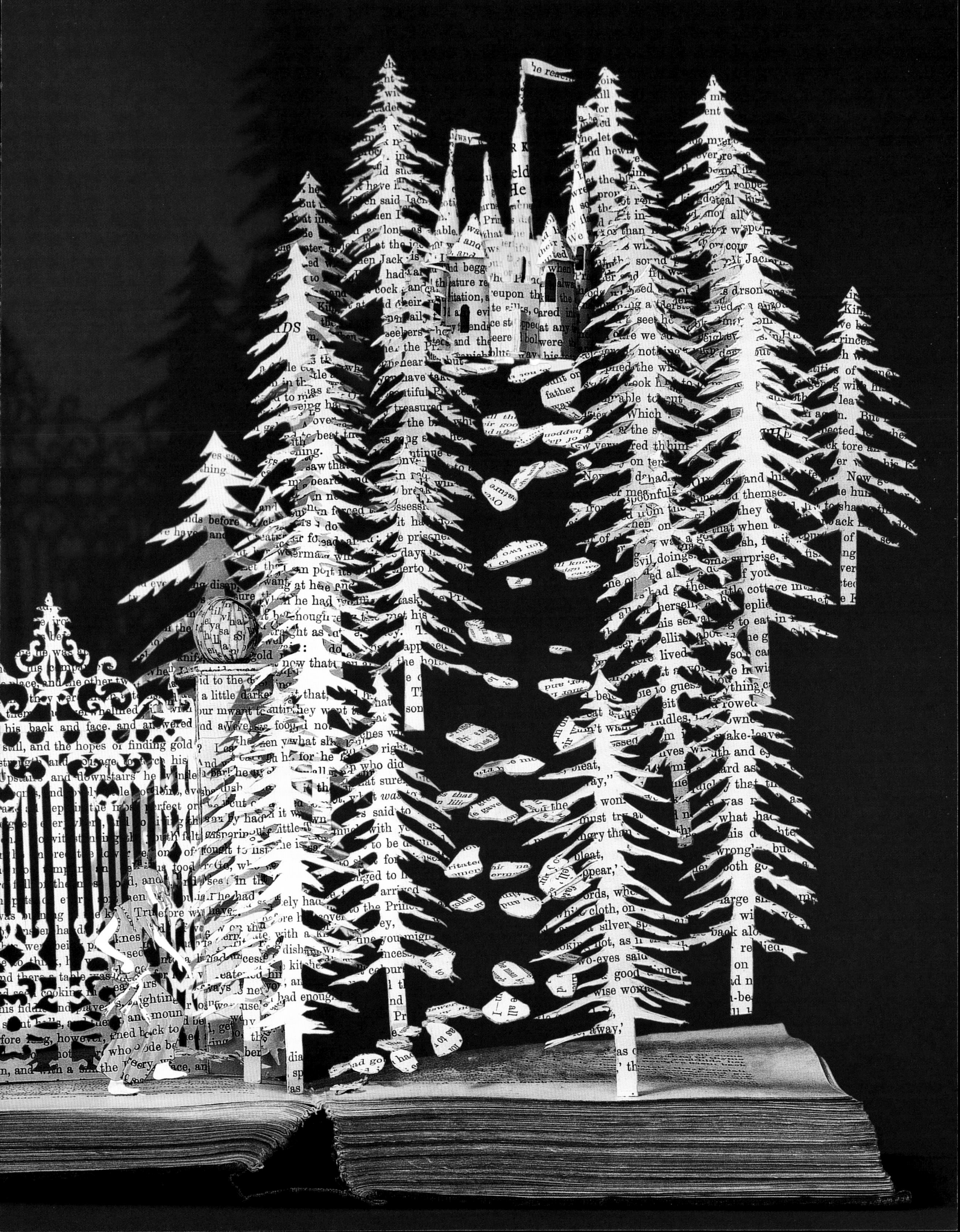

"Well," thought the old queen when she heard this, "We shall soon see if she is a real princess."

The queen went into the sumptuous spare bedroom, pulled the white sheets from the four-poster bed and placed just one pea – a teeny-tiny, tiddly green pea – right in the middle of the mattress. Then she piled ten big fat mattresses and four woolen blankets on top of the teeny-tiny, tiddly green pea. Finally, on the very top of the tottering pile, the old queen spread a fine cotton sheet, one white silk quilt, one delicate lacy coverlet and a plump feather pillow. It looked very soft indeed.

The bed was so high it almost reached the ceiling. So the queen asked her footman to fetch a ladder because the princess would need one to get into such an extraordinarily tall bed. And that was where the princess slept the night.

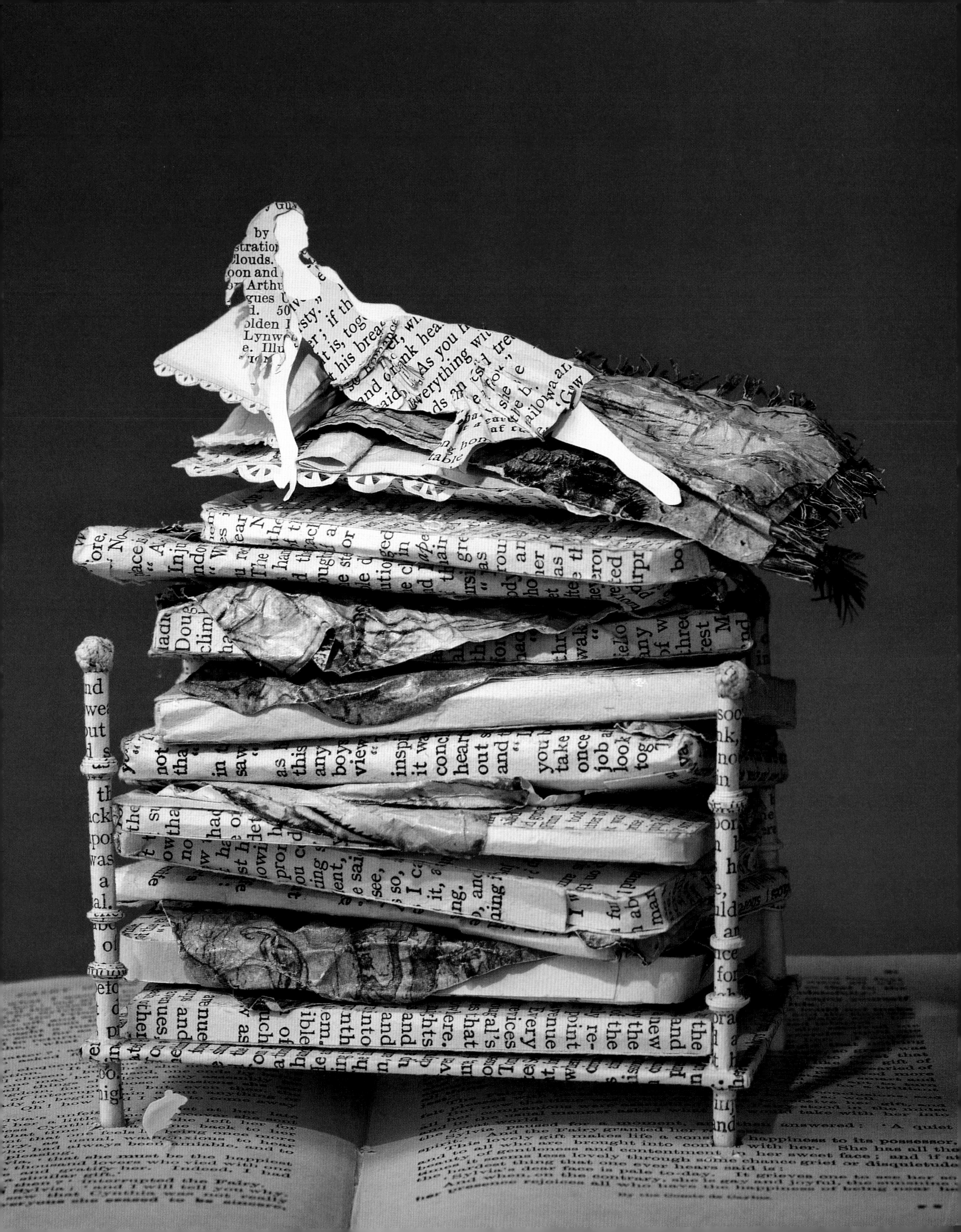

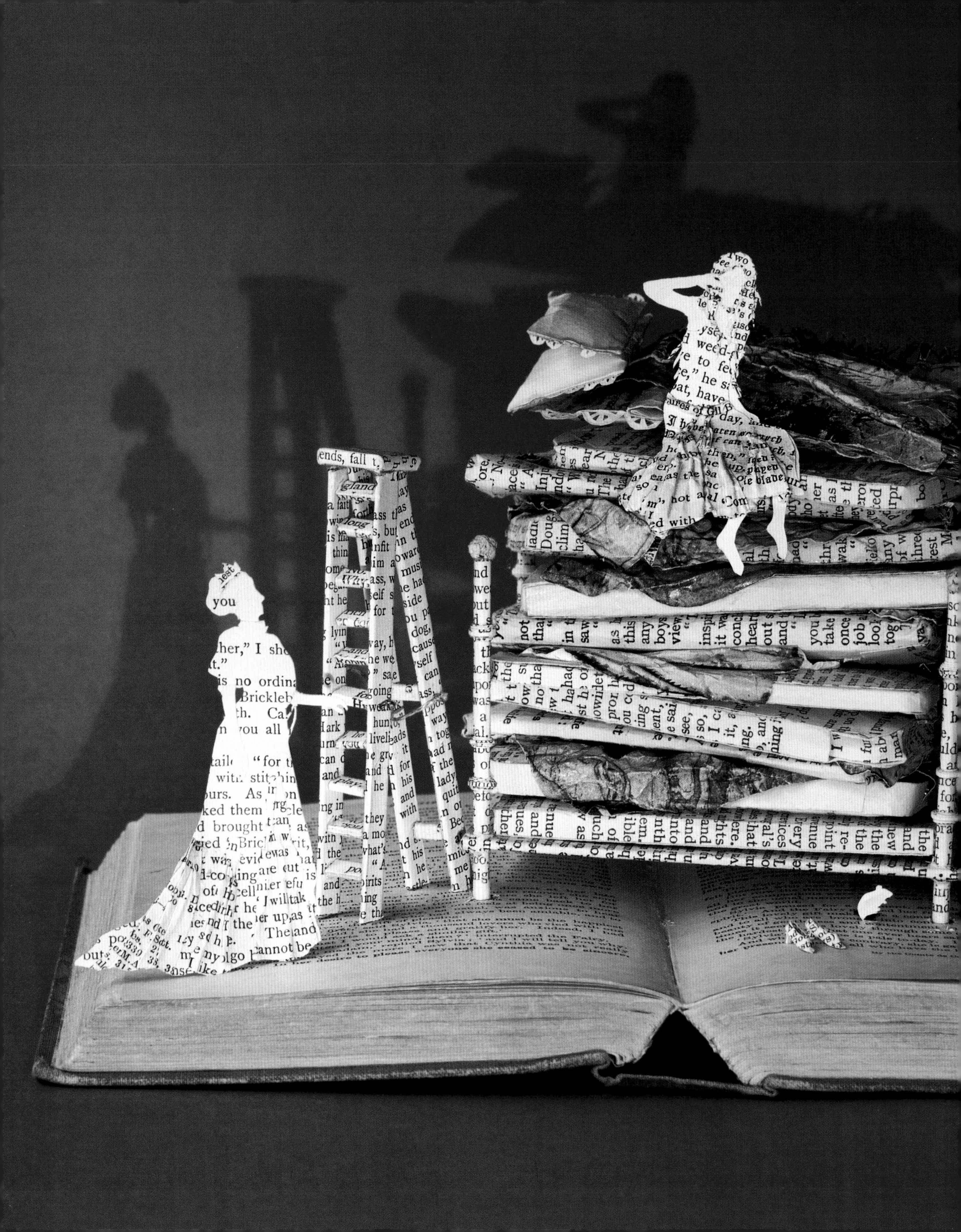

In the morning, once the sun had risen, the old queen went to the princess.

"How did you sleep?" she asked.

"Oh, shockingly! Terribly! Appallingly!" said the princess. "I hardly slept a wink all night long."

The princess yawned and stretched and rubbed her eyes sleepily.

"Why not?" asked the queen, looking up at her. "Were you not comfortable? I made the bed especially for you and I thought that so many mattresses and covers should make for a very soft bed."

"Thank you for your kindness," said the princess, "but heaven only knows what was under the mattress. I lay on something so very hard and so very solid that I'm black and blue all over."

Now the old king and queen and the prince knew without a single, teeny-tiny, tiddly doubt that the princess was a real princess. She had felt the pea through ten big fat mattresses, four woolen blankets, a fine cotton sheet, one white silk quilt, one delicate lacy coverlet and a plump feather pillow. Only a real princess would be that sensitive.

The prince and princess were married and had the most splendid wedding cake, all covered with sweet green peas.

And the pea was put in a glass case in a museum, where you can see it for yourself. That is if a prince – a prince who is searching for a real princess – hasn't stolen it.

Snow White

ONCE UPON A TIME, when snow was falling like feathers from the sky, a young queen sat by a window sewing. She pricked her finger and three drops of red blood fell on the snow. The queen looked at the drops and said, "I wish I could have a child with skin as white as snow, with rosy-red cheeks and hair as dark as night." And indeed she had such a baby girl. She called her Snow White.

Soon after, the queen died. Within a year, the king married again. His new wife was beautiful but cruel and vain. Every day she stared into her magic looking-glass and asked, "Mirror, mirror on the wall, who is the fairest of them all?"

"You are," replied the looking-glass.

All the while, Snow White was growing into a beautiful young girl. One day, the new queen asked her looking-glass, "Mirror, mirror on the wall, who is the fairest of them all?"

But this time the mirror replied, "Snow White."

The queen turned green with envy. She ordered the royal hunter to take Snow White to the forest.

"Kill her!" she cried. "Bring back her lungs and liver to me."

The hunter dragged Snow White into the forest, but his courage failed him. He abandoned Snow White and killed a deer instead, taking its lungs and liver back to the queen.

Snow White was terrified and ran through the forest until it was dark. Then she fell asleep on the hard ground.

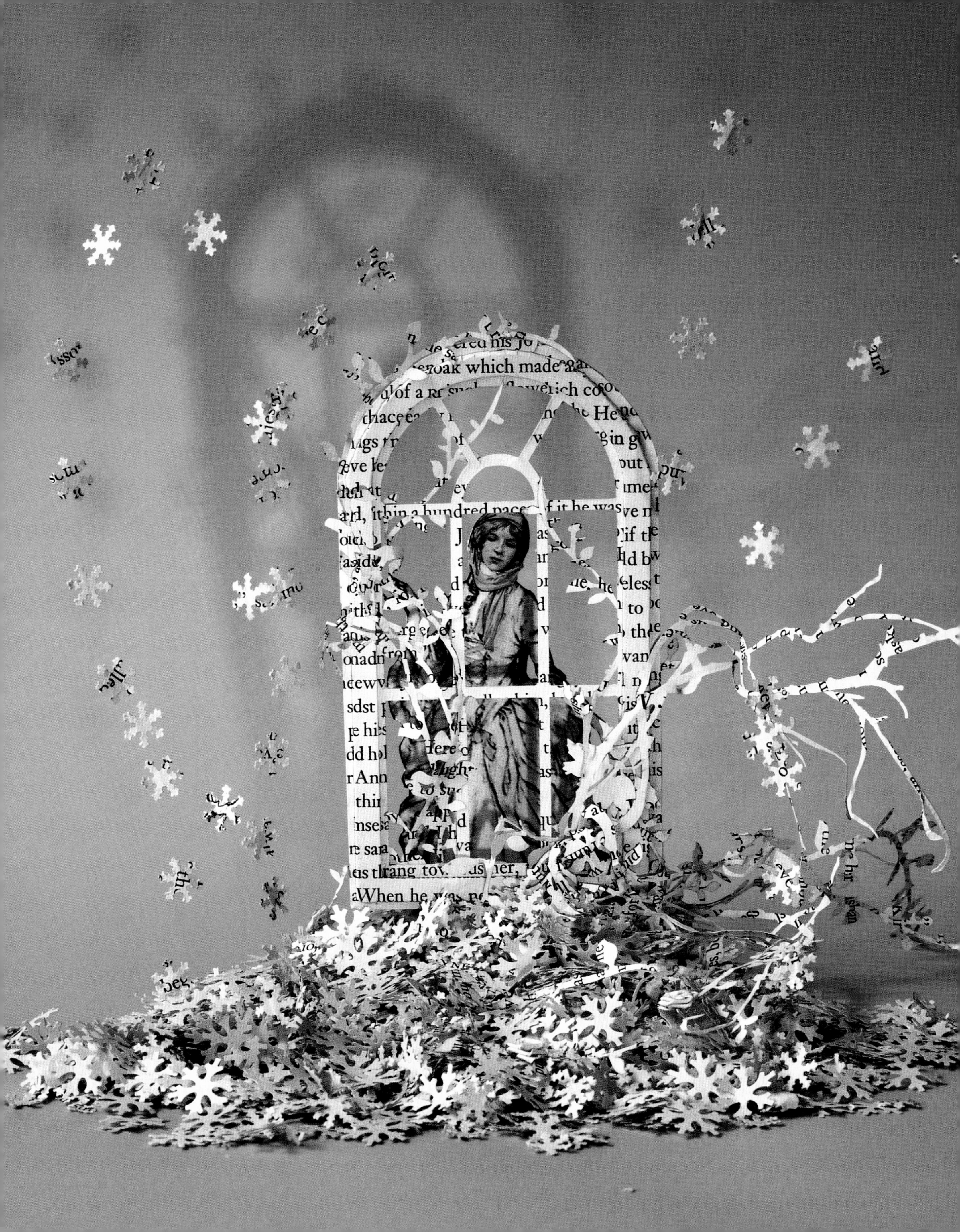

The next morning, Snow White awoke to see a cottage in the distance. Inside the cottage, there was a small table.

"What small plates and bowls and cups!" she exclaimed.

She ate a crust of bread from each plate, took a spoonful of soup from each bowl and drank a drop of water from each cup. Upstairs, there were seven small beds. Snow White lay down on each bed but none suited her, until at last the seventh bed was just right and she fell asleep.

At dusk, seven dwarfs returned to the cottage from the mountain where they worked as miners.

The first said, "Who's been sitting on my chair?"

The second said, "Who's been eating my bread?"

The third said, "Who's been using my spoon?"

The fourth said, "Who's been eating my soup?"

The fifth said, "Who's been using my cup?"

The sixth said, "Who's been drinking my water?"

And the seventh said, "Look who's sleeping in my bed!"

"Oh, heavens!" all seven cried.

In the morning, when Snow White awoke, she saw the seven little men standing round the bed. At first she was frightened, but they were friendly.

"What is your name?" they asked.

"My name is Snow White," she answered.

"And why are you in our house?" they asked.

"It is a sad story," said Snow White. She told them all about her stepmother and the hunter and how she had run and run until at last she had come to their home.

The dwarfs gathered together and talked to each other.

Then one said, "If you tend to our cottage when we are mining in the mountain, and if you keep everything spick-and-span and clean and tidy, you can stay with us and you will want for nothing."

"Oh, yes!" said Snow White. "I would like to stay here with all my heart."

So each morning the dwarfs went to the mountain to mine copper and gold. Each evening Snow White had their supper ready and waiting on the small table. And every day the dwarfs warned Snow White, "Do not open the door to strangers."

Meanwhile, the hunter returned to the castle with the lungs and liver of the deer and told the queen that they belonged to Snow White. The hunter got his rich reward and the delighted queen rushed to her magic looking-glass.

"Mirror, mirror on the wall, who is the fairest of them all?"

"Over the hills, where the dwarfs dwell, Snow White is alive and well. She is the most beautiful of them all," replied the looking-glass.

The queen went green with envy, then scarlet with rage. She would find Snow White!

The wicked queen put a poison apple in a basket of red apples and dressed up as an old peasant so that no one would recognize her. Before long she was at the door of the cottage.

"Good day to you," said Snow White through the closed door. "Who are you?"

"I am a poor old woman selling ripe, red apples," said the queen.

"But I must not open the door to strangers," replied Snow White.

"What a good girl you are!" said the old woman. "Let me give you one of my apples."

Snow White opened the door and took the poison apple. She bit into it and fell down as if dead.

"Ha!" the wicked queen cried. "Now *I* am the most beautiful!" She ran through the forest, but tripped on her shawl, tumbled into a swamp and disappeared without a trace.

At sunset, when the seven dwarfs came home, they found Snow White lying on the floor. They tried and tried to wake her, but Snow White remained still and lifeless. All seven of them sat around her body and wept for three long days.

"We cannot bury her in the dark earth," they said. So they made Snow White a crystal coffin and carried her into the forest where they laid her on a bed of leaves.

Snow White looked as though she were asleep – her skin still white, her cheeks rosy-red and her hair as dark as night.

Soon after, a king's son came to the forest and saw the coffin. When he saw how beautiful Snow White was, he fell in love.

"Let me take her to my castle," he said to the dwarfs. "I will give you whatever you want."

"We will not part with her," the dwarfs replied.

"Let me have her," the prince pleaded. "For now I have seen Snow White, I cannot live without her."

The dwarfs took pity on the prince and gave him the coffin. But as the prince lifted it up, he stumbled over a tree stump and the piece of poisonous apple fell out of Snow White's mouth.

Snow White opened her eyes.

"You are alive! You are with me!" said the prince, full of joy. "Come to my father's palace, Snow White, and be my wife."

Snow White went gladly with the prince to his castle, which was near to the dwarfs' cottage.

Soon the couple were married with great splendor and the seven dwarfs were their guests of honor.

And Snow White and the prince lived happily ever after.

Rapunzel

O<small>NCE</small> <small>UPON</small> <small>A</small> <small>TIME</small>, there was a husband and wife and their baby. The wife was sick in bed and every day she grew thinner and thinner. Nothing in the world could cure her except for the tall, green herb that grew in her neighbor's garden. The herb was called Rapunzel, and the wife begged her husband to steal a bit from their neighbor.

But the garden belonged to a wicked witch. One day, the witch caught the husband stealing her herb and screeched, "You must give me your child as payment for my herb!"

"No!" shouted the husband in horror. But the witch snatched the baby away.

"She's mine now," the witch declared.

The couple were heartbroken. They watched their daughter over the garden wall as she grew into a beautiful child with long golden hair. The witch called her Rapunzel.

he thought
his bow
sunset he
piness that
seemed heard
ing heard
path that
you could

od in his
new not
ntry he
at if the
as there
another.
men say
new
ith new
y, many
home.
he ones

hardly
sweeter
their nos
birds circle
rocks nor tree
knowing it, for
the souls of them.
So he went on wit
great lake, with a lovely can
bank of the lake was a can
were two shining paddles.
The chief jumped straight into
pushed off from the shore, when to
following him in another canoe exactly lik

When Rapunzel was twelve years old, the witch locked her in a tower with no door or staircase. Rapunzel was lonely and spent her days singing to the birds.

Every day, the witch came and called, "Rapunzel! Oh, Rapunzel! Let down your hair."

Rapunzel dropped her golden braid out of the window and the witch climbed up to give her food, then slid away.

A few years later, a prince was riding past. He heard the sound of sweet singing. "What a beautiful voice," he thought. He rode to the tower but could see no door. Soon the witch came and called, "Rapunzel! Oh, Rapunzel! Let down your hair."

The prince watched unseen. Then when the witch left, he called, "Rapunzel! Oh, Rapunzel! Let down your hair."

The braid tumbled down and the prince climbed up to the top of the tower.

"Who are you?" Rapunzel asked in surprise.

"I am a prince," he said. "I followed the sound of your sweet singing." He sat with Rapunzel at the window and told her about the world outside.

"I promise to come again," he said. And so he did and so they fell in love.

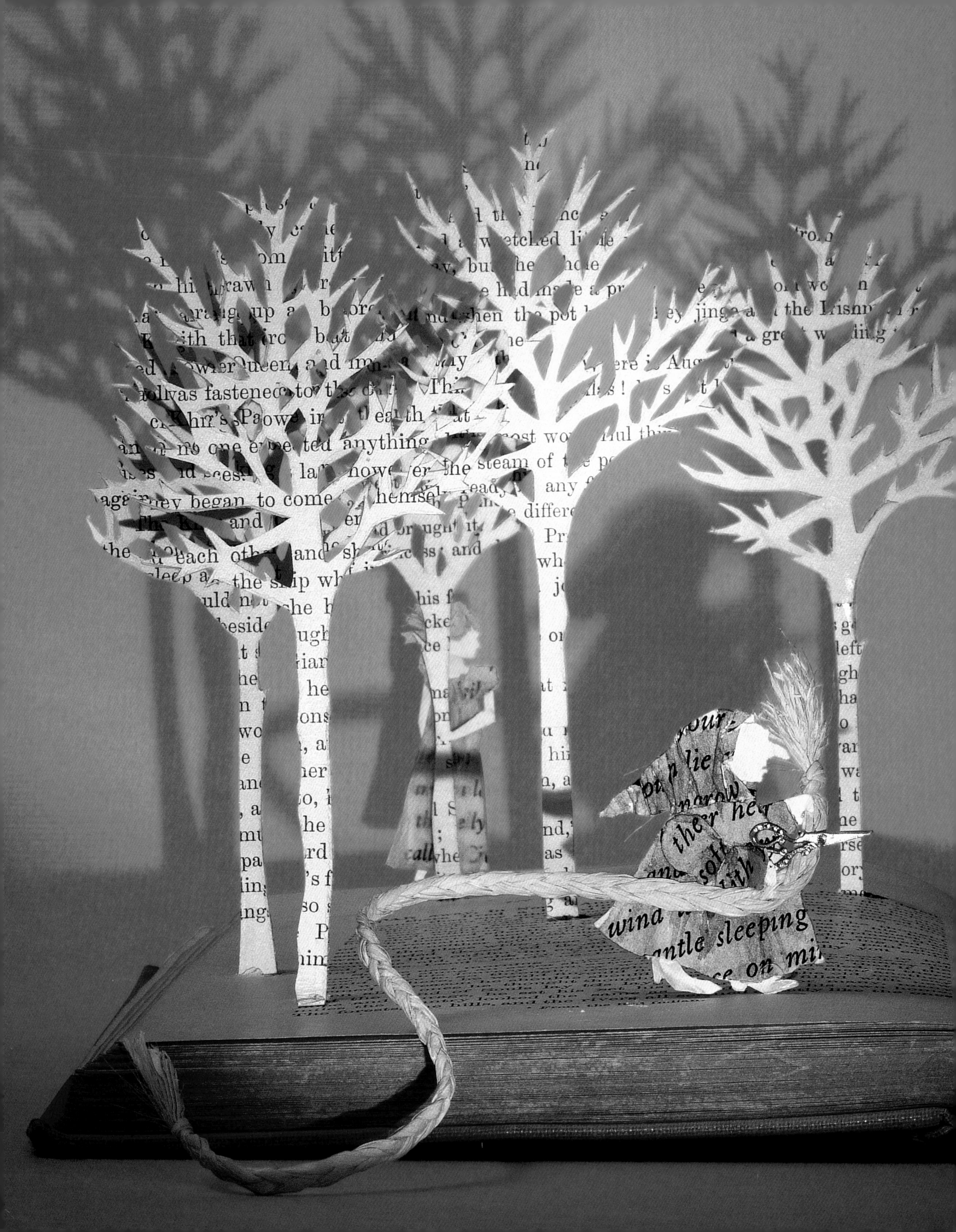

One sunny day, Rapunzel asked the witch, "Why are you so very heavy when you climb my hair? You are so much heavier and slower than the handsome prince who comes to visit me in the tower."

"A handsome prince comes to visit you!" the witch shrieked in rage. She took Rapunzel from the tower and dragged her into the deep dark forest. The witch took a pair of silver scissors and hacked at Rapunzel's long golden braid. Then the witch grabbed the hair and ran as fast as her little legs would carry her back to the tower.

Rapunzel stood among the trees. She had nothing to eat and nowhere to sleep. She was all alone in the deep, dark forest.

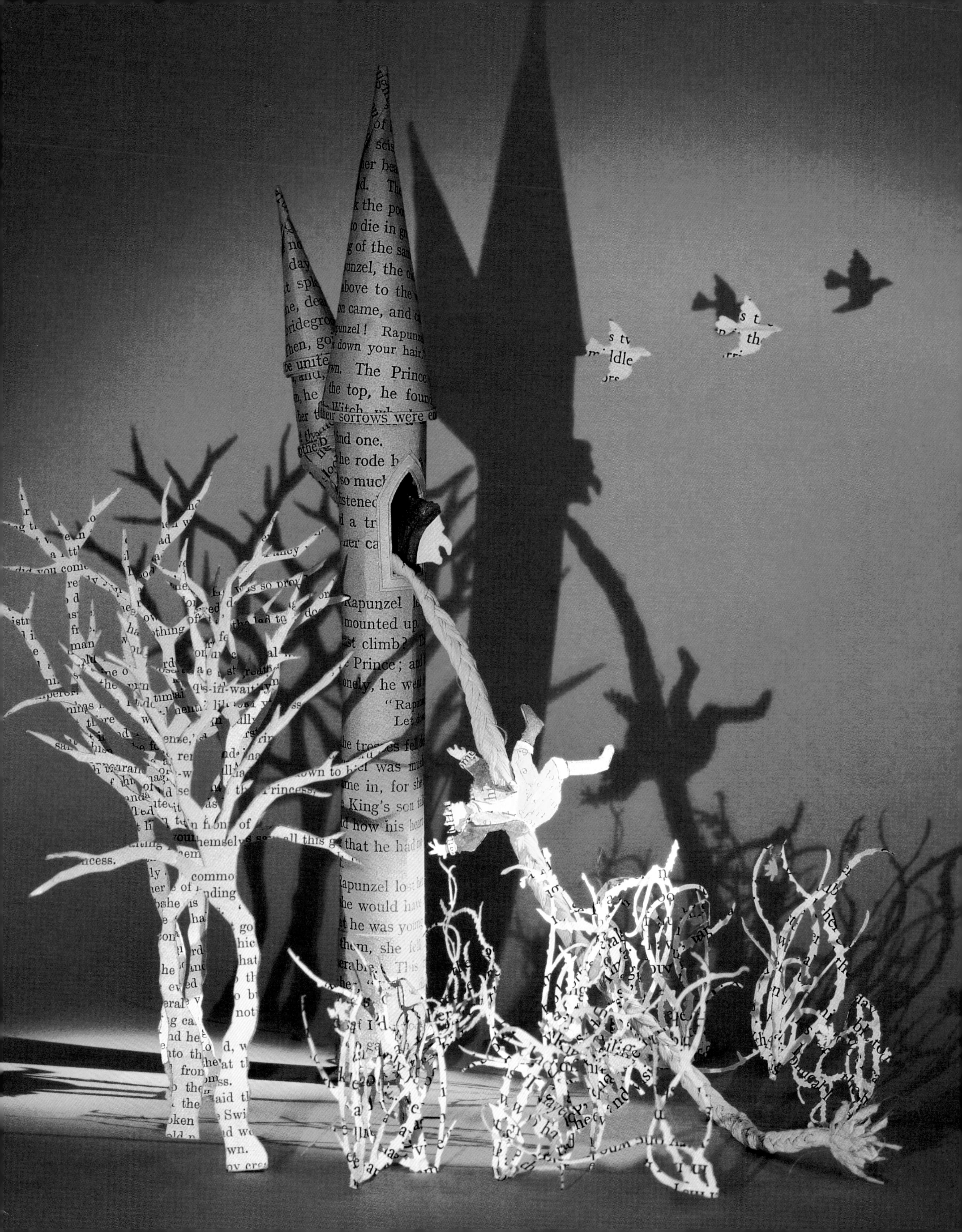

Later that evening, the prince came to the tower.

"Rapunzel! Oh, Rapunzel!" he called. "Let down your hair."

The witch knotted Rapunzel's braid around the window frame, threw it down and the prince climbed up.

When the prince reached the top of the tower, the witch screamed, "You will never see Rapunzel again!" She clawed at his eyes and the prince fell from the tower and landed in a thorn bush. His eyes were scratched and he stumbled blindly into the forest.

After three days wandering, the prince heard sweet singing.

"Rapunzel?" he called. Rapunzel came and kissed him and his eyes were healed. He could see again.

The prince took Rapunzel to his palace, where her parents awaited. Rapunzel and the prince were married and lived happily ever after. And the witch was never seen again.

was, and
king's s
prince w
dventure,
moment
wood when
gave way of the
avenue to the ca
aw none of his
hind him again
he did not cease
always valiant.
ne into a spacious o
ight have frozen the
fright
refused all
dea wh
d treas

Sleeping Beauty

Long, long ago, and far, far away, there was a king and a queen who lived in a splendid castle. Every day the queen said, "All I want is a child," but a child didn't come.

One day the queen was lying in a deep, warm bath when a great fat frog leaped out of the water.

"Your Majesty," it croaked. "Soon you will have a daughter."

"A daughter!" exclaimed the queen and smiled.

And so it came to pass. Within a year, the queen had a baby girl. The king was so delighted that he ordered a feast to celebrate.

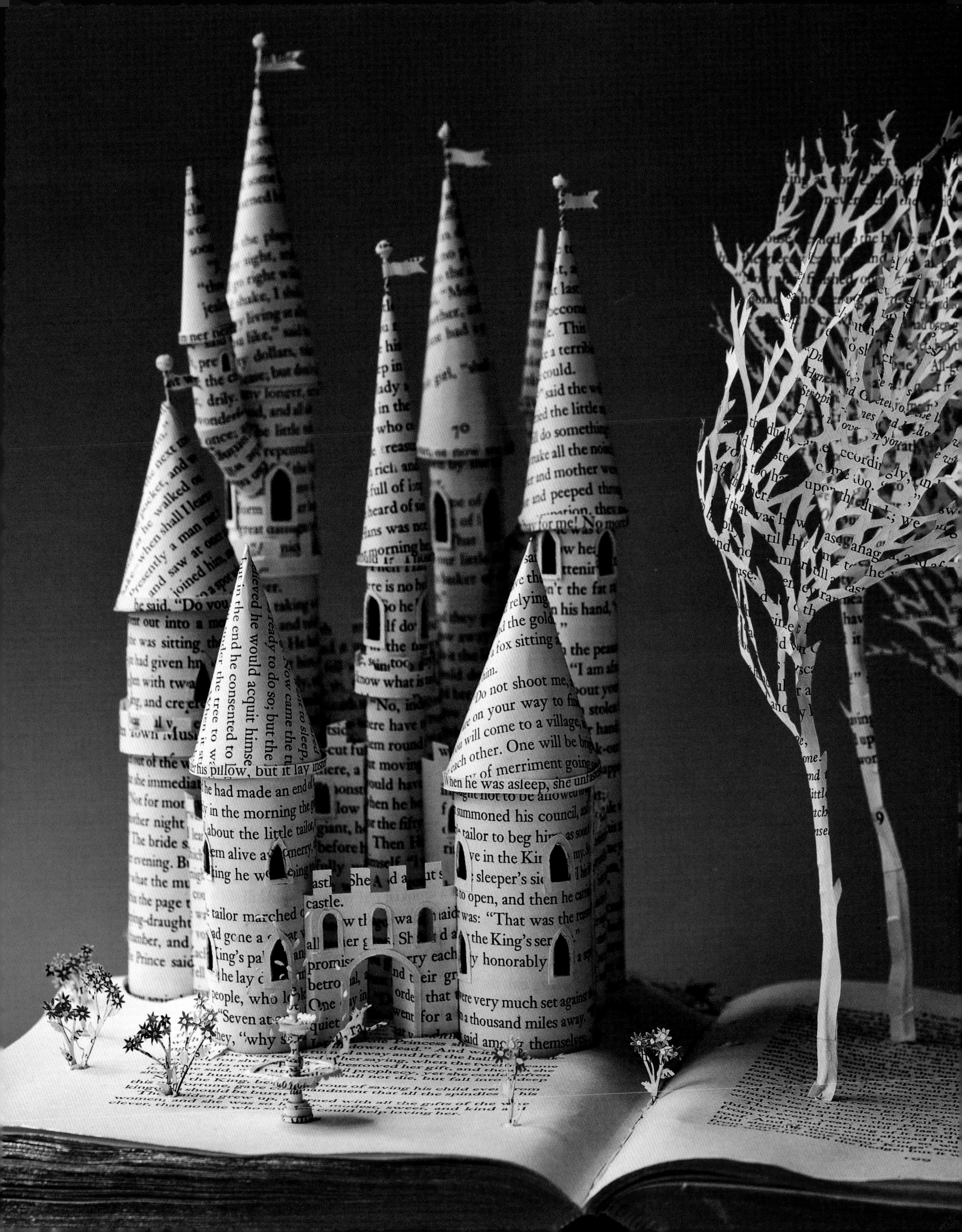

"Invite all the lords and ladies, dames and knights," commanded the king. "And the wise women of my kingdom shall be the princess's fairy godmothers."

But there were thirteen wise women and only twelve silver plates so the thirteenth wise woman was not invited.

The feast was splendid, the hall magnificent and the food delicious. At the end of the feast, each wise woman gave the baby princess a magical gift. The first gave the gift of goodness, the second the gift of beauty, the third gave wealth, and the fourth gave kindness. When the last was about to give her gift, the thirteenth wise woman – the one who had not been invited – burst into the hall.

In a terrible, terrifying voice, she said, "In her fifteenth year, this princess will prick her finger on the needle of a spinning-wheel and she will die!" Then she turned and left.

The hall fell silent.

Fortunately, the twelfth wise woman had yet to give her gift. Although she could not undo the wicked curse, she could soften it.

"The princess won't die," she promised, "but she will fall asleep for a hundred years."

The king cried, "Burn all the spinning-wheels in my kingdom. At once!"

The princess grew up and was blessed with all the magical gifts the eleven wise women had bestowed upon her. She was beautiful, kind and full of grace. The wicked wish was forgotten.

And so it happened that on the princess's fifteenth birthday, the king and queen went out hunting and the princess was left alone. She wandered through the castle until she came to a tall tower. She climbed its narrow winding staircase and at the top found a small door. In the door was a rusty key. She turned the key, and inside the dark room, there was an old woman.

"Good day to you, old woman. What do you have there?" the princess asked, for she had never seen a spinning-wheel before.

"It's a spinning-wheel for spinning wool," the old woman replied.

"And what is that?" asked the princess as she reached out to touch the spindle. But no sooner had she touched the wheel than she pricked her finger on the needle. The princess fell on to the bed and into the deepest sleep.

The wicked wish had come true.

As the princess slept, so did the entire castle. The king and queen, returning home, fell asleep on their golden thrones. The horses fell asleep in the stable. The cook, who at that moment was reaching out to punish the kitchen boy, fell asleep, and so did the kitchen boy. The dog slept on the floor, and the cat too. The flies slept on the wall. All the servants, wherever they were, fell asleep. And the roast stopped sizzling when the fire stopped flickering.

Around the castle grew the thickest thorn trees, which reached higher and higher with every passing year, until only the tops of the tall towers could be seen.

Throughout the land people spoke of the sleeping beauty. Many princes tried to enter the castle, but they got caught in the thick thorns and could never free themselves and died.

Almost one hundred years later, a handsome prince was riding through the land when he met an old man, who told him about the castle behind the wall of thorns, and the sleeping princess within.

"Her name is Briar Rose," said the old man. "She is said to be as beautiful as she is graceful." And then he told the prince what had happened to the other princes before him.

"I am not afraid," the prince said. "I will see this princess."

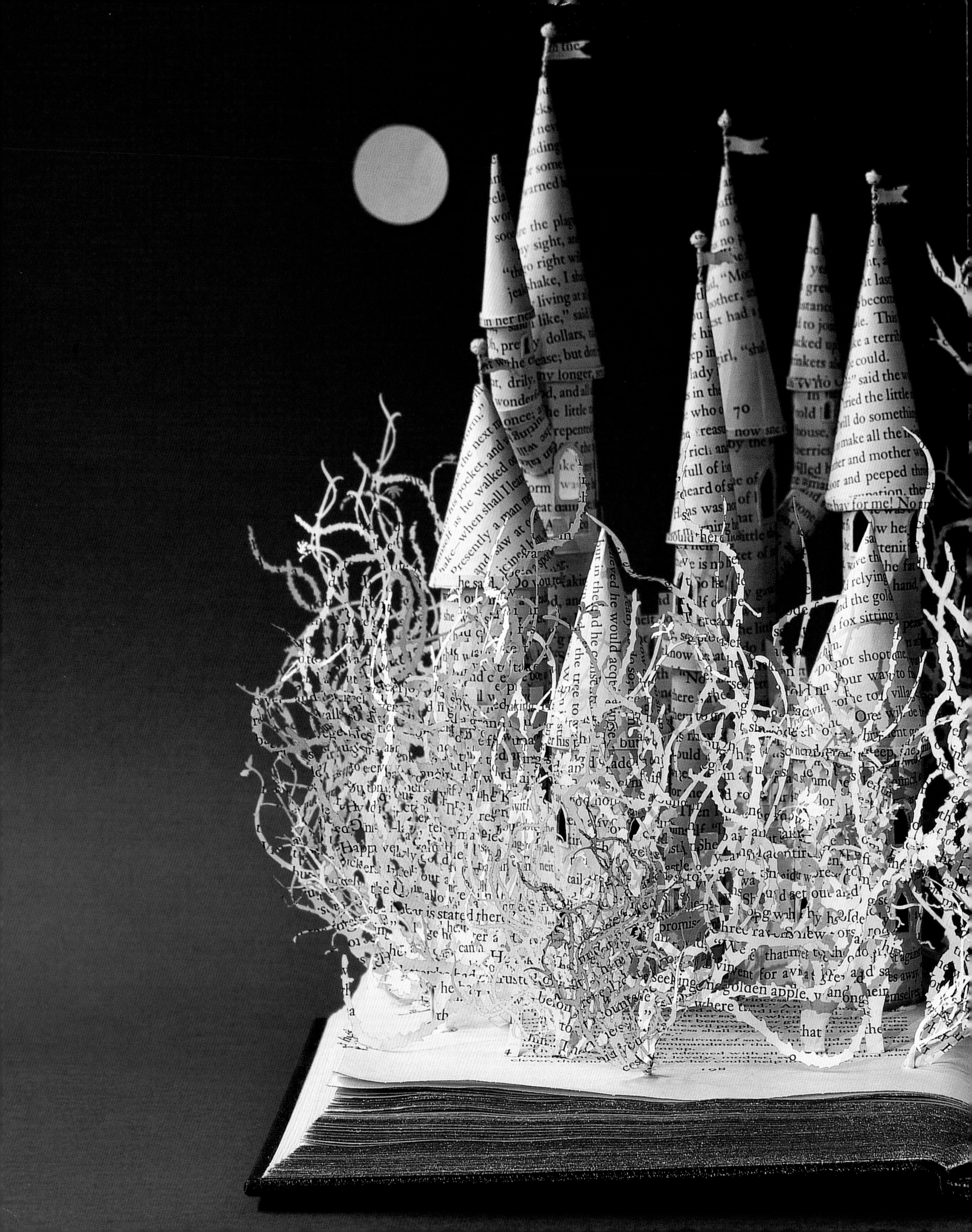

It so happened that on the day the prince reached the castle, exactly one hundred years had passed. As the prince cut at the forest of thorns with his axe, the thorns magically turned into beautiful flowers that swayed aside to make a path for him to enter.

Once inside the castle, the prince saw the king and queen asleep on their golden thrones, the horses asleep in the stable and the pigeons on the roof with their heads under their wings. The flies slept on the wall. The dog slept on the floor, and the cat too.

Everyone was sleeping; everywhere was silence. As the prince walked further and further into the castle, all he could hear was the sound of his own breath.

At last the prince came to the tallest tower. He climbed the narrow winding stairs until he reached the small door with the rusty key. He turned the key and opened the door. And there lay Briar Rose asleep on the bed. He was overcome with her beauty.

The prince kissed Briar Rose. She awoke and looked at him kindly.

Together the prince and princess left the small room in the tall tower and walked through the castle.

The king and queen awoke and were astonished. The horses in the stable shook themselves and the dog jumped up and chased the cat. The pigeons took their heads from under their wings and flew to the fields. The flies buzzed around. The kitchen boy dodged the cook. The fire in the hearth broke into flames and the roast sizzled again.

And so the prince married the princess. The wedding was splendid and the feast was delicious. And they lived happily ever after.

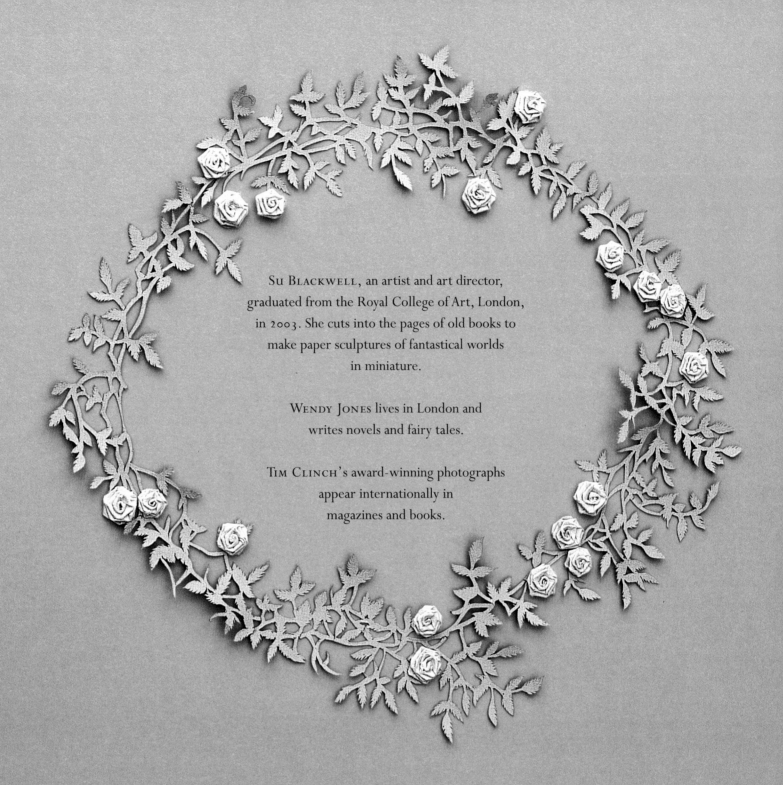

Su Blackwell, an artist and art director,
graduated from the Royal College of Art, London,
in 2003. She cuts into the pages of old books to
make paper sculptures of fantastical worlds
in miniature.

Wendy Jones lives in London and
writes novels and fairy tales.

Tim Clinch's award-winning photographs
appear internationally in
magazines and books.

Paper sculptures by Su Blackwell
Retellings by Wendy Jones
Photographs by Tim Clinch, with the exception of
the front and back cover images by Aaron Hayden

The Fairytale Princess © 2012 Thames & Hudson Ltd, London
Paper sculptures © 2012 Su Blackwell

First published in 2012 in hardcover in the United States of America by
Thames & Hudson Inc., 500 Fifth Avenue, New York, New York 10110

thamesandhudsonusa.com

Library of Congress Catalog Card Number 2012930270

ISBN 978-0-500-65006-6

Printed and bound in China by Asia Pacific Offset Ltd